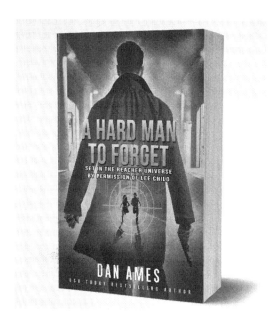

Book One in The JACK REACHER Cases

THE JACK REACHER CASES (THE MAN WHO STRIKES FEAR)

THE JACK REACHER CASES #9

DAN AMES

FREE BOOKS AND MORE

Would you like a FREE copy
of my story BULLET RIVER and the chance
to win a free Kindle?

Then sign up for the DAN AMES BOOK CLUB:

AUTHORDANAMES.COM

THE MAN WHO STRIKES FEAR

The Jack Reacher Cases #9

by

Dan Ames

1

Special Agent in Charge Edward Giles had lost his rage. Road rage, that is. For years, the drive home to his house on Long Island had been characterized by frequent shouting and obscene gestures.

For people who knew him, it would have been a revelation.

As an FBI agent in the New York office, he was known by his colleagues as being a very even-keeled, well-tempered investigator. Calm, methodical, and easily able to study the most heinous crimes imaginable with a serene sense of detachment.

Perhaps that was why he frequently lost his temper driving home. It was because he'd spent the day bottling up his emotions and the commute provided the perfect outlet to release his tensions. That way he wouldn't kick the dog and shout at his wife the minute he walked in the door.

The rage, however, had completely disappeared two weeks ago.

He hadn't started seeing a therapist. Or popping antidepressants.

Instead, he'd announced his retirement and given the office his two weeks notice.

Now, he didn't mind the traffic at all because he was in a good mood. As much satisfaction as he'd had over the years as an agent at the Bureau, the amount of good he'd done, there had still been pressure.

He was not one of those men who hated their jobs. Who cursed their co-workers behind their backs and dreamed of the day they could tell everyone to go to hell and storm out of the building.

All that being said, he was happy to be ending his career. He and his wife had a condo in Florida, a boat tied up at a marina down there and Giles planned to spend nearly every day out on the water, fishing, swimming, or just tooling around and enjoying the sun, warm weather and fresh air.

Perhaps for the first time since he was a kid, he would have a tan.

It was amazing how much faster the drive went sans the anger. It seemed like in no time he was pulling into the driveway of the four-bedroom colonial house with immaculate landscaping and a commanding view on the hill.

The home was Giles' pride and joy. He was a man who liked order and had found it therapeutic to putter around the house on weekends, fixing things, sprucing up the exterior, squaring everything away. In his line of work, there weren't always neatly tied endings. Usually, just the opposite. It was perhaps one of the reasons he found yardwork and home renovation so refreshing. There was always a very clear before-and-after.

Giles parked the car and entered the home from the side door and felt the prongs of a Taser slam into his neck.

There was no time to defend himself.

His muscles went rigid and then everything collapsed.

He was still conscious but felt enormous pain and he was immobile, save for twitching and jerking as the voltage continued to wreak havoc on his muscular and nervous systems.

Giles felt himself being dragged into the living room where he saw his wife pinned up against the wall.

The image made no sense to him.

Nancy was naked and her arms and legs were spread.

Giles realized she wasn't pinned to the wall.

She'd been nailed to it.

Blood seeped from each of her hands and feet, down the beige wall, the very wall he'd respackled, primed and painted over the winter.

Whoever had done this to his wife had cleared away the furniture and torn the artwork from the wall.

Because there was a big space next to his wife.

He knew the space was for him.

His mind and body were in shock, but he was still an FBI agent and his training was kicking in. He fought to assess the situation.

Giles got his first look at the assailants. There was more than one of them, at least three. Probably men, dressed in black clothes, with plastic around their shoes and they wore surgical gloves.

And masks.

Giles felt his clothes being ripped from his body and then one of the men lifted him up against the wall while another one with a nail gun drove nails into his hands and feet. He tried to fight but he had no strength.

He wasn't sure when he started screaming but a scalpel had been produced and they were cutting off parts of his body. He saw one of the men holding something that had been sliced from his body and then the man approached his wife.

Giles couldn't see what happened because he was losing blood at an astonishing rate and he felt himself floating above the scene.

He couldn't see anything.

Couldn't feel anything.

And then he was gone.

One month.

It had been exactly one month since Lauren Pauling had officially sold her private investigative firm in New York, and moved in with Michael Tallon.

Tallon's little adobe ranch near the Nevada/California border, within a stone's throw of Death Valley, had been her home for the past thirty days.

It was their anniversary.

Of course, it hadn't been without incident.

A bizarre psychological experiment at a military base nearby had led to multiple murders and the worst kind of violence one could imagine. Some of it had even taken place here, inside Tallon's home.

They'd recovered, naturally. Tallon was an experienced Special Ops soldier and had seen more than his fair share of gore. Pauling, too, was no babe in the woods.

So they'd moved on.

Now, Pauling had cooked a meal she knew Tallon would love. Baby back ribs on the smoker behind Tallon's house. They'd been slow-cooking out there for the better part of the afternoon. Inside, she had some gloriously indulgent homemade biscuits with sautéed green beans.

In the fridge, Pauling had a bottle of Tallon's favorite beer, ice-cold and at the ready.

Pauling heard him pull into the driveway, and then he entered through the side door. She had a bottle of beer ready for him.

In his hand was a big bundle of red roses.

"Ah, you're just full of surprises," she said. They embraced and she kissed him, then handed him the beer.

"Flower for the lady. Beer for the gentleman," she said. "Look at us, we've fallen perfectly into society's roles."

"Not exactly," Tallon said, pointing at Pauling's service weapon on her hip. Ever since the murders, she'd been a little reluctant to be too far from her gun, especially when she was home alone. It was odd as she'd lived a long time in New York and never felt that way.

Tallon understood, and let it drop.

She never tired of looking at him. Tall, broad shoulders, narrow waist and a ruggedly handsome face. He was a selfless and enthusiastic lover. They fit together perfectly, both anatomically and personality-wise.

"I thought guys never remembered anniversaries," Pauling said, neatly slicing the stems of the roses and dropping them into a silver vase.

Tallon stepped up behind her and slid his arms around her waist. "Most guys probably don't," he said. "Then again, most guys don't have you."

They kissed, made their way to the bedroom and made love. Afterward, Pauling went to the backyard and checked on the ribs while Tallon poured himself another beer, and uncorked a bottle of wine for Pauling.

He joined her outside.

She was putting the last of the barbecue sauce on the ribs, just a hint as she'd applied a homemade rub and didn't want to overpower it, when her cell phone rang.

Tallon took the sauce and the basting brush from her so she could answer.

"Hello?" she said.

Pauling sipped from her glass of wine and listened.

No, she thought.

Pauling looked up and saw Tallon watching her, his eyes wide with concern for her.

She continued to listen numbly as the news bounced around inside her consciousness.

Her old boss at the FBI in New York, a man named Edward Giles was dead.

He'd been murdered.

The first to arrive at the Giles residence was a Long Island cop. He'd been on the force for ten years and had seen less than five murders in his time with the department.

Nothing prepared him for what he saw at the home of the Giles residence.

All of that Hollywood crap about cops being tough, and putting menthol above their upper lip to counteract the smell of people butchered?

It didn't work.

Officer Lampkin took one look at the carnage on display, a man and a woman literally nailed to the wall, sliced in a million places, the man's genitalia cut off, and he ran for the door.

He barely made it back outside where he thoroughly regurgitated his lunch of a Reuben sandwich from the D'Monico deli that he ate at least once a week.

Now, he knew he would probably never touch it again.

Lampkin called for backup and made sure his vomit

hadn't disturbed the crime scene. In fact, he grabbed an orange cone and placed it over the pile of his former lunch.

His stomach was still roiling and he couldn't stop thinking about what he'd seen.

It had started so innocently. An anonymous call had come into dispatch complaining that fireworks had been heard near the Giles home, and Lampkin had been the nearest officer. He'd parked, walked around the home and then seen that the side door was open.

Inside, he thought he saw blood on the floor so he'd made the mistake of entering the house.

Now, he waited for backup and wondered what in the hell he'd just seen.

He closed his eyes and saw the dead bodies.

But there had been something else, written in blood on the wall.

Two words.

Lampkin squeezed his eyes closed and tried to remember what they'd said.

His stomach was still gurgling and he felt unsteady on his feet.

And then it came to him.

The two words.

For Reacher.

4

The first FBI agent to arrive at the Giles household was a man named Arnie Steele. He'd been with the Bureau for over twenty years and was the highest-ranking special agent on duty when the call came in.

The New York office's director was now being informed of the situation and would no doubt be on his way shortly.

For now, Steele was in charge.

He entered the house and instantly remembered the layout. He'd been here several times. Once for a poker night several years back, the other just a friendly gathering of Bureau friends. They were the kind of casual summer get-togethers that used to happen regularly in the good old days, but that now hardly ever took place.

Steele remembered that Giles had been an amateur pit master and enjoyed making heaps of barbecue for guests. Cold beer, and lots of laughs, is how Steele remembered the place.

Now, he stood in no small amount of shock at the sight of his friend and colleague nailed to the home's living room wall. Giles had clearly been mutilated, as had been Giles' wife, Nancy. Steele remembered her as being the extrovert of the two, always ready with a laugh or a quip.

Steele knew that Giles was about to retire, and that his caseload had basically been wound down to nothing. His first thought was that the murders had nothing do with Giles' job, because none of his fellow agents' recent cases had indicated violence of this nature.

Maybe it was a home invasion. Or a robbery.

The entire New York FBI office would work on this case, and find out who was responsible.

The forensic team had also arrived and now Steele stepped aside, letting them take their photographs, measurements and notes.

Steele had been through the rest of the house and had already spotted the writing on the wall.

For Reacher.

It had been written in blood.

Steele had no idea what or who a Reacher was, but he was going to find out.

And then he was going to find the people who had murdered his friends, and make them pay for what they'd done.

5

"Bad news?" Tallon asked.

He had seen Pauling's reaction as she listened on the phone, and he even noticed her body jolt, as if someone had sucker punched her in the solar plexus.

"Yeah," she said.

Pauling told him that an agent from the FBI's New York office had just told her that a man she'd worked with off and on for many years was dead.

"He was murdered," she said.

Tallon went to her and put his arms around her.

"I'm sorry," he said. "Was he on the job?"

"I don't have all the details yet, but it sounds like he was killed in his home."

"Maybe a domestic issue?" Tallon asked.

Pauling shrugged her shoulders. It was a helluva thing, she thought. It was how life often worked. Here she was, relaxed, fresh from making love, cooking a celebratory meal with a man who she was clearly in love with, and boom. Out of the blue, death.

The news notwithstanding, Pauling and Tallon brought the ribs inside, and ate their meal.

"This is incredible," Tallon said, after he'd polished off yet another rib.

"Thank you," she said.

He looked at her, saw the resignation in her eyes.

"You're going back," he said.

Pauling nodded.

"I have to."

"Yes, of course," Tallon said.

They cleared their plates, loaded the dishes into the dishwasher, and Tallon poured them each a finger of whiskey.

Tallon sat on the leather couch in the living room, the late evening's shadows reaching into the room. The desert was outside, full of things that came to life in the night, avoiding the day's heat.

Pauling sat next to him, curled up against him. Felt his warmth.

"We just can't catch a break, can we?" she asked. "First, the ordeal with the rogue soldiers, now, a murder back in New York."

"It kind of goes with the territory, right?" he said. "In our line of work, this is what happens. Investment bankers? They get emergency calls about currency devaluation and everything goes to hell."

She leaned back and looked at him.

"Currency devaluation? Listen to you."

"I have no idea what it means," he said with a grin. "It just sounded like something investment bankers would deal with."

She nodded. "I don't think I'll be gone too long. The funeral will probably be in a couple of days, and then I may hang around for a little longer just to find out what's going on."

Tallon felt a twinge inside. He loved Pauling more than any woman he'd ever been with. He was happy she was here, but he knew how easily things could change. She could go back to New York, get roped back into some kind of investigation, and find her old life comforting. Maybe reconsider what she'd done.

Tallon was smart enough to know that he couldn't control that kind of thing.

He leaned in and kissed her.

"Hey, do what you need to do. I'll be here."

Pauling smiled and kissed him back.

"I know," she said.

They rode in a Mercedes-Benz motor home designed for overnight stays. It was black with tinted windows and had a bed, bath and small kitchen. There was a sink, a microwave, a refrigerator and a flat screen television. A storage cabinet held a variety of industrial-grade cleaning supplies. The bed, which was never used, was home to a collection of weapons. There were multiple handguns, assault rifles, knives, cutting tools and a nail gun.

Off to the side was a collection of plastic gloves, booties and rolls of clear plastic sheeting.

The men didn't sleep in the vehicle, instead they chose cheap motels and paid cash.

The purpose of the motor home wasn't for habitation, rather, as a place to clean up between jobs. It afforded privacy when the team preferred not to be seen in public.

They'd plastered the back with fake stickers from national parks and even had a bicycle attached to the rear of the vehicle. Depending on the location and setting of their "projects" they would often rent a car, paid for in cash, to get from the motor home to the job site and back again.

Now, the team had finished cleaning up after their job on Long Island and the big Benz moved down the road quietly.

Its next destination was known to only one member of the team.

The others would wait for instructions.

And then follow them to the letter.

Pauling settled into her first-class seat on the direct flight to New York.

She felt a strange mixture of emotions. She was torn between the abrupt departure from Tallon and the daily experience of what life was now like, and a surprisingly powerful tug of yearning about returning home.

"Home" was a term she still felt wasn't clearly defined. Her apartment in New York was technically her home. But she'd joined Tallon out West and had felt the first tendrils of roots begin to dig into the dry, desert soil.

And then the call.

Edward Giles.

Pauling remembered him fondly as a mild-mannered, methodical FBI agent. He avoided office politics and focused on the case at hand, treating colleagues with equal respect. Giles always seemed like the kind of guy who might be a little different once he was out of the office – maybe yelling at people in traffic, or letting loose occasionally on the weekend. Pauling vaguely remembered going to his house once for a cookout and meeting his wife, Nancy. They'd made a cute couple, clearly balancing each other out personality-wise.

But as far as the Bureau went, Giles was one of the best she'd worked with. She remembered him quite fondly because he had defended her once, when a fellow agent had discriminated against her. The guy, Pauling couldn't even remember his name, had made a derogatory comment or two. He abruptly stopped, and later she learned that Giles "had a word" with the man.

Now, he was dead.

Pauling shook her head. Giles had probably been retired, or close to it. People often talked about their retirement, what they were going to do when they were done with their professional lives. She wondered how many folks actually lived their dreams.

Pauling considered herself, too. After all, she was now somewhat retired. Or at least, out of work. She'd sold her private investigative firm and was now "seeking new opportunities."

Whatever the hell that meant. She was now independently wealthy, thanks to the outrageous amount her competitor had paid for her firm. She really didn't have to work again, but knew that she would.

Detective work, investigation, it was in her blood and always would be.

Pauling put it out of her mind and let her mind wander for the rest of the flight. When she touched down, the plane jolted and Pauling thought to herself, welcome to New York.

She took an Uber back to her apartment, and was pleased to see that the cleaning service was doing a fine job. The space was a loft, with high ceilings, natural wood and comfortable furnishings.

The state-of-the-art alarm system was working just fine.

It was something she'd had to invest in a while back when one of her cases hit a little bit too close to home. She'd already checked the web-based video and knew that nothing had happened out of the ordinary.

Pauling unpacked, dug out a bottle of wine and poured herself a glass as she wandered aimlessly around the place.

So different than the desert and Tallon.

Looking out the window she saw a slightly overcast day, with people walking quickly along the sidewalk, taxis honking at each other, and the eternal hum of the city. She felt relaxed, pleased to be back in "her" space.

Eventually, Pauling made her way into her home office and turned on the computer. She waited and watched it come to life, then opened up her email where she found a message from one of her former colleagues.

The woman who'd sent her the message was a good friend, but the message contained a forwarded message from Arnie Steele.

Pauling groaned.

She'd butted heads with Steele on more than one occasion.

But now, she studied the message. Steele had sent it to a select few within the Bureau who had probably been tasked with helping find out who had murdered Giles.

Pauling gasped as she saw what it contained.

An autopsy.

Giles had been brutally murdered.

His wife tortured.

Worst of all, no one knew why.

8

The FBI team assembled in the office's biggest conference room. Despite their collectively vast experience with crime, the hardened agents were all in a state of shock.

Details about the murder of Giles and his wife had leaked throughout the office and everyone had wanted to play a role in catching and punishing those responsible.

Reluctantly, SAC Steele had assembled a slightly larger group than he had originally intended. They were all present, save for William Tisdale, Director of the New York's Bureau.

Just when Steele was about to kick off the meeting, Tisdale entered. He was a short, taciturn man with silver hair in a neat buzz cut. He wore neatly tailored suits, rimless eyeglasses and a Patek Philippe watch on a black alligator band.

He sat down at the head of the table and nodded to Steele.

Tisdale had always been a man of few words and Steele

often wondered if it was his nature, or if he preferred to limit the amount of things he said that were 'on the record.'

Despite his reticence, Tisdale was a man who knew how to get things done. While not overtly political, his elegant manner simply prevented him from engaging in the skull-duggery so often present in bureaucracies.

Steele respected his superior and knew that he had control of this investigation.

"Okay, here's what we know," Steele said.

He walked the team through the preliminary autopsy findings, not shirking the worst of the descriptions, but not elaborating any more than necessary.

Steeled focused his gaze on a balding man with a red goatee.

"Sullivan, I want you, Mendez and Jackson to pore over all of Giles' cases for the past five years. Bring everything up to date. Where the players are now? Was anyone released from prison? A conviction overturned? New evidence? Appeal granted? Anything new or unusual, pounce on it."

Sullivan nodded.

Steele turned to a woman with short, honey-colored hair, gunmetal gray eyeglasses and prominent cheekbones. Her name was Wyman.

"Agent Wyman, I want you, Rawlins and Gerike to focus on the same things, except I want them to be cases *not* related to Giles. Anything new with our active cases? Or cases going back the past five years. Meaning – maybe somebody wanted to hit the Bureau, and they just picked Giles at random."

"Got it," Wyman said.

There was a pause.

It was Tisdale who broke the silence.

"*For Reacher*," he said. Technically, it wasn't a question, but Steele knew what the Director wanted.

"I'm handling that," Steele answered, his voice unable to disguise his anger.

9

I t was a clear, blue-sky morning with only a firm, chilly breeze to take the edge off of what would ordinarily be a beautiful day.

For Pauling, she was glad the cold wind was bearing down on the cemetery and the funeral procession.

It somehow didn't seem right to have a friend lowered into the ground on a picture postcard kind of morning. Frankly, Pauling wished it was brutally cold and raining so that the sight of Giles and his wife being lowered into the earth would almost feel like protection for them.

Instead, it felt as if they had been victimized yet again. The living allowed to savor the warmth of sun, the sight of an azure sky overhead, while the dead remained oblivious.

Pauling turned into the wind, let it blast her with its cold and although not a religious person, she prayed for the souls of the dead, and asked the powers-that-be to help law enforcement catch the bastards and put them away for life.

She sensed someone by her side and turned. FBI Special Agent Rose Wyman nodded to Pauling.

The two of them had gotten to know each other years ago at the Bureau. Wyman was at least ten years younger than Pauling, and Pauling had been a bit of a mentor to the woman. In fact, it had been Wyman who'd gotten the message to Pauling about Giles, along with the autopsy report.

"Pauling," Wyman said.

"Hell of a thing," Pauling answered. "Any progress?"

To the outside observer, their interaction might have seemed distant, maybe even a little cold. But they were both FBI agents, one current, one former. The businesslike demeanor rarely changed.

"Roles assigned, that's it so far."

"Steele?"

Wyman nodded. "Yep."

Pauling and Steele had been competitors during Pauling's time at the NY Bureau. It had also been a slightly different time, when women were still fighting for their footing and Pauling had been on the front lines of that battle. She often joked that she had "trained" Steele, although it had probably cost her in the long run.

Pauling could never be certain, but she assumed as Steele rose above her in the Bureau, that he had actively stunted her career growth.

She saw him standing to the left of the priest. The Gileses didn't have any family, save for a sister who lived in Europe. There was no one present other than friends and co-workers.

Steele looked a little older, but Tisdale looked exactly the same. Pauling almost smiled – Tisdale would probably look the same at ninety years old as he did now.

Pauling felt eyes on her and glanced back at Steele. He was staring directly at her.

She nodded at him.
He didn't nod back.

10

T he Mercedes-Benz motor coach parked outside the chain hotel and the men inside quietly discussed their strategy.

They had made the drive to the outskirts of Atlanta and their target was only a dozen miles away, just outside the upscale community of Buckhead, on the north side of the city.

The big vehicle was equipped with high-speed Internet and the team leader had downloaded a dossier on the target, complete with high-resolution photographs, video, schedules and an analysis of response times should any alarm be sounded.

The information had been supplied to him.

The alarm system in question was middle-tier, meaning it would not be a challenge to the men inside the Benz.

A plan of attack was put into place, weapons dispensed and placed into innocuous-looking roller bags, and the men took turns checking into the hotel, leaving a gap of at least thirty minutes between each.

They would not reconvene until approximately three in

the morning, so they could reach the target by 3:30. It was their favorite time of day to attack, when guards were lowered.

The last thing the team leader did was to check the supplies.

Plenty of nails for the high-powered nail gun.

And more than enough plastic gloves and booties.

11

"Pauling."

She turned and saw Arnie Steele approaching her. He was dressed in a black suit, white shirt and black tie. He was powerfully built, and Pauling knew he was a workout fanatic. Everything Steele did, he tended to do it with maximum intensity. He had a reputation for wearing out agents who were in the unfortunate position of working beneath him.

The service was over and Pauling had been about to climb into her vehicle and head back to the city.

"Hello Arnie," Pauling said. She decided to be casual, just because she could. No longer a part of the Bureau, she felt no need to continue organizational protocol. Plus, she knew it would probably get under his skin.

"I didn't expect to see you here," he said. "I'd heard you'd moved out West."

Pauling wasn't surprised Steele had kept tabs on her. The sale of her firm and the eye-popping numbers were fairly big news in the world of private security and law enforcement circles. She was a little disappointed he'd obviously kept tabs on her personal life, too.

But that was his point. He was trying to get under her skin, too.

"Giles was a good man," she said, ignoring the line of his conversation.

"He was."

They stood in silence for a moment as a vehicle passed them. Pauling caught the sight of Tisdale in the passenger seat, looking at her. He nodded as they passed.

"Wyman fill you in?" he asked. Pauling knew she had to be careful. Steele could be an asshole, she didn't want to get her friend in any kind of trouble.

"No, NYPD actually," she said. It was a lie, but she actually did have a lot of contacts within the NYPD and it was plausible.

She doubted Steele would buy it.

"How long are you in town for?" he asked.

"Long enough," she said. "Are you going to catch them?"

"Of course," he replied.

He hesitated as if he wanted to say more, but he didn't.

Pauling opened the door to her vehicle and glanced at him.

"Make sure you do," she said.

enry Lee had long come to terms with being the sole African-American in a neighborhood as white as rice. He often felt like the token black, for there had been no recriminations, no rocks thrown through the windows. In fact, everyone had been as nice as could be.

Perhaps it was because he, too, was wealthy. The Bentley in the driveway. The fact that he was a bachelor without kids. But deep down, he felt like he'd been sheltered from any kind of racism by the fact that he was the only one.

Now, if suddenly, an influx of blacks into the neighborhood could be attributed to him then he was pretty sure there would be problems.

But for now?

He was fine.

Golden.

Henry was in his home office where he spent the majority of the day analyzing spreadsheets on his computer. He was a financial advisor for a select group of very wealthy clients who had found him by referral only. If one were to look for Henry Lee's company online or in the phone book, you would be out of luck.

In fact, he rarely used the actual name of his service. It was only needed at tax time when he had to file his return.

Other than that, his clients knew him by his name, as opposed to a business entity.

Now, he studied the financial charts with an acumen that was well beyond ordinary. Henry had always been gifted with numbers and once he'd been introduced to the financial markets, it had all made sense to him. So much so that by the time he was in his early twenties he was so well off that he would never have to work again.

But that was the thing.

This wasn't work to him.

It was fun.

It was what he was born to do.

The numbers enveloped him like a warm blanket and he became oblivious to everything around him.

In fact, he had no idea that someone had entered his home.

Or that they were now in his office.

When the man stepped up behind him and clamped a hand over Henry's mouth, he was caught completely by surprise.

When a second man entered the room with guns, knives and sheets of plastic, Henry Lee knew that he was a dead man.

He just didn't know why.

13

Michael Tallon studied the sit rep – or situation report – from a friend of his working private security in Australia. It seemed that a splinter terrorist group had set up shop down under and was planning a series of potential attacks on American tourists.

The Australian government had reached out to Tallon's former colleague and asked for a proposal to provide supplemental surveillance and possible intervention, should the need arise.

Tallon's buddy had submitted a proposal with an outrageously high fee that the Australian government had instantly approved.

Now, his friend was trying to put together the right team and the first person he had reached out to was Tallon.

The sit rep was very thorough, as he had expected. His former colleague's name was Caldwell and his nickname was "All Well" because of his meticulous nature. When Caldwell did something, he did it very, very well.

Hence, the moniker.

Tallon was able to discern that the job required he travel to Australia and spend about a month there, maybe two, and for his time, he would be paid approximately one hundred thousand dollars.

It was a premium contract, that was for sure. Especially as the potential for armed conflict was fairly low. Ordinarily, a job with this kind of money always meant live fire and active hostiles would be involved.

It was the kind of job he would have previously accepted on the spot.

But now, it was different.

Because of Pauling.

Tallon closed the document from Caldwell and opened the autopsy report Pauling had shown him.

He was certainly no stranger to torture and murder, but the crime scene images of the FBI agent and his wife back in New York gave Tallon pause.

They were spectacularly brutal.

A viciousness rarely seen in civilian circles. Overseas? In terrorist camps and on the front lines with groups like Al-Qaeda and ISIS, this kind of thing was fairly ordinary.

Tallon wondered about Pauling and if she would get involved in the investigation. He hoped not. These were some really horrible people, and she had been out of the FBI game for quite awhile now.

Listen to yourself, he laughed. Worrying about Pauling. He knew she was more than capable of handling herself in any kind of situation.

Being in love with her had momentarily clouded his thinking.

Tallon closed the autopsy report and opened up his email.

First, he sent a note to Pauling briefly explaining the job offer and his decision.

And then he sent a note to Caldwell informing him he was accepting the gig.

14

They met for drinks at a bar a short cab ride from Pauling's apartment.

Wyman showed up with that weary expression Pauling knew so well. A day at the Bureau could drain a person mentally, physically and emotionally. There had been long days after which Pauling would get home, look in the mirror, and see the same kind of bone-deep fatigue Wyman was displaying right now.

Not to mention when an agent was killed in the line of duty, there was a sense of survivor guilt. And anger. Plenty of anger.

"What are you drinking?" Pauling asked as she caught the eye of the bartender. She had already ordered a dirty martini and started a tab.

"Grey Goose martini with a blue cheese olive," Wyman told the bartender who placed Pauling's drink in front of her.

Limelight was a retro kind of bar, with mostly craft cocktails and a limited bar menu. It primarily served office drones who preferred to wait for rush hour to end before heading home rather than fighting traffic or other riders on the subway or on commuter trains.

Right now, the bar was fairly full. Mostly well-dressed professionals, probably a lot of brokers from Wall Street.

Pauling had chosen a quiet high-top table opposite the entrance. It was the best spot in the bar to be able to have an actual conversation, as opposed to yelling at each other.

"Long day?" she asked Wyman.

"Very."

"Here's to Giles," Pauling said. They clinked glasses and each took a long drink.

Wyman let out a long sigh.

Pauling held up her hand. "Look, you don't need to tell me anything. I know how the Bureau is, and Steele in particular. So if you want to keep whatever you're doing under wraps, that's find with me."

"Don't be ridiculous," Wyman said. "What the hell else are we going to talk about? Football?"

"The new concussion protocol?" Pauling asked.

They both laughed.

"Yeah, I'm in charge of Option C," Wyman said, her voice somewhat bitter. In terms of FBI vernacular, Option C would be one of the less important, or less likely to be productive, avenues of investigation.

In other words, it was usually the angle that would almost certainly lead to nothing, but that simply had to be eliminated. And it was usually assigned to the least senior agent.

"And Steele assigned himself Option A," Pauling said.

"Of course. I'm responsible for any unusual occurrences *not* related to Giles. New prison releases, bail jumpers, new threats against the Bureau, etc."

"Well, it's always possible," Pauling said. "Look at the

bright side – at least you're doing something for Giles. I'm not."

"Yeah, I just wish I was working on Giles' cases. That's where we're going to find the bad guys. There's no way it was an anonymous hit on a generic FBI agent. They went after Giles and his wife for a reason. A very specific reason."

"Agreed."

"It's just a little odd, though," Wyman ventured. "Giles was about to retire. He had been winding things down for quite some time. The last few cases of his had been fairly mundane. Insider training. White-collar espionage. Wire fraud. All with pretty low stakes."

"Nothing white-collar or low stakes about what they did to him."

"That's what's odd."

A group of men in nearly identical suits entered the bar. Pauling pegged them as attorneys.

"Could be tangential," Pauling pointed out. "Maybe it wasn't the bad guys he convicted, but their victims. Maybe they didn't feel the FBI did a good enough job punishing the people who screwed them over."

"Yeah, could be," Wyman said. Her strong jaw was nearly clenched and Pauling wanted to tell her to relax, but she didn't. That's how it was working at the Bureau. High stakes. High pressure.

There were rumors about Wyman's sexual orientation. She was single. Not married. And never talked about dating. Pauling suspected she was gay, but never asked. It was none of her business.

Pauling missed this part of her work at the Bureau. The spitballing. The testing out of theories. Teamwork. Even though politics sometimes interfered at the office, most of the time it was set aside for the greater good.

"Who knows, maybe Steele will uncover something Giles was working on that will throw the investigation into a whole new light," Pauling offered, trying to be positive.

"Oh, Steele's not working on that. That's Option B."

"What exactly is Option A then?"

Wyman hesitated and Pauling knew despite their friendship, the woman for the first time was wondering how much she should share.

"There was a detail not included in the autopsy and the crime scene reports. Withheld from everyone except for the core team."

Pauling nodded. The Bureau, and law enforcement in general, did it all the time. It was usually done to rule out phony call-ins who claimed credit. And, to sometimes make the killers think they were one step ahead. Or, in some cases the detail was too gruesome to be made public.

Pauling wondered in the case of Giles if it was one or all of the above.

"You don't have to–" Pauling said.

"Two words, written on the living room wall in blood," Wyman said.

She paused and looked into Pauling's eyes.

"For Reacher."

15

T he team leader stood in Henry Lee's office, studied the dead man nailed to the wall. He'd been stripped, tortured, and his body desecrated in ways that were only limited by the dark imaginations of his men.

Blood was everywhere, which was the point.

The rest of the men had gathered their weapons and tools, and were now waiting in the generic rental car which they would use to transport their tools back to the motor home.

The murder had gone just as planned. Henry Lee had screamed like the others, although it had been muffled by the duct tape across his mouth. The team leader had understood what the dying man was asking.

What do you want?

I'll give you anything!

The idiot had no way of knowing they didn't want anything. At least, nothing that Henry Lee could provide voluntarily.

Now, before he left, he knew he had one job left to do.

Still wearing the latex surgeon's gloves, he dipped one finger into Henry's Lee rapidly drying blood and wrote two words on the wall.

For Reacher.

16

Pauling had done something slightly out of the ordinary and ordered a second martini. She couldn't help herself; Wyman's description of what had been written on the wall of the Giles crime scene had shaken her to the core.

For Reacher.

What the hell did that mean?

Jack Reacher?

"What's wrong?" Wyman asked.

Pauling quickly recovered. "I've been out of the game too long," she lied. "I still can't believe this happened."

She had no intention of telling Wyman about her history with Jack Reacher. At least, not yet.

They stayed at the bar and talked at length about the Bureau, stories involving Giles, and Pauling shared a few Arnie Steele tales, as well. But the truth was, Pauling couldn't concentrate. All she could think about was how and why Reacher's name had been dragged into the crime scene of her former colleague.

By the time they finished their drinks, Pauling still wasn't closer to an answer.

She paid for the drinks at the bar and then they each hailed a cab.

Pauling gave Wyman a quick hug, which seemed to surprise the other woman. Wyman promised to keep her up to speed as best she could. Pauling told her not to jeopardize her standing at the office.

Back at home, Pauling grabbed a bottled water from the fridge and drank half of it in one long pull.

For Reacher, as in, revenge?

Someone had killed Edward Giles in revenge for something Reacher had done? Well, Pauling had to admit that there were probably a lot of people who wouldn't mind getting revenge on Reacher. He was a one-man wrecking crew and had probably put dozens of bad guys in hospitals. But what did that have to do with Giles? Or the New York FBI?

Pauling wandered into the living room and thought about the time she'd spent here with Reacher. How they'd made love in the bedroom multiple times.

Were they crossing paths again?

For Reacher.

The only conclusion Pauling could come up with was that maybe there'd been a case that involved both Reacher and Giles.

If so, that would be Steele's job to find out. He'd assigned himself Option A and any link between Reacher and Giles would be the top priority, in Pauling's estimation.

It must have been the same conclusion Steele reached, too, otherwise he wouldn't have assigned it to himself.

Pauling weighed her options.

Obviously, Wyman hadn't known about Pauling's

connection to Reacher. Did that mean Steele didn't either? He'd known about her recent trip out West. Was it possible the FBI didn't know?

The case she'd worked on with Reacher had been at a time when she'd already left the Bureau.

If they did know, well, that didn't matter. They could contact her or not.

If they didn't know, though, was it her obligation to volunteer the information? And what information did she have exactly?

She didn't know where the hell Reacher was.

No one did.

Half the time, Reacher didn't know where he was going.

So, Pauling couldn't help them in that regard.

Plus, she hadn't seen him in years. Other than the case they'd worked on which by now was very old news, she had no other information.

Thinking objectively, Pauling couldn't come up with a good reason to volunteer her history with Reacher, except for the fact that it would possibly get her involved with the investigation of Giles' murder.

But even that was iffy.

Steele would most likely get whatever information he could from her and then toss her to the side. Pauling couldn't blame him, she probably would do the same thing in his situation.

She glanced across her living room toward the short hallway that led to her home office.

In a previous case years ago she'd helped an IT specialist get out from under a white-collar theft charge by proving he'd been framed. As part of her payment, he'd figured out a way for Pauling to maintain her access to the FBI's internal databases. Not technically illegal, it was simply that her log in and password credentials were updated thanks to her profile being hidden on the Bureau's server and listed as active.

She ducked back into the kitchen, started a pot of coffee, and went into her home office. Pauling turned on the lights and started her computer.

There was little chance she would find something the team at headquarters had overlooked, but that wasn't her goal.

Pauling wanted to find out how Reacher was involved.

And if she needed to warn him.

17

W hile Henry Lee had been a virtuoso with numbers, spreadsheets and mathematical calculations, he hadn't been very good with a broom and a mop.

Which is why he'd employed the services of one Jasmine Karnos, a woman from Bulgaria who'd been recommended by one of his neighbors.

Lee had figured she was probably in the country illegally, but when she cleaned his house, it was spotless and smelled like the lobby of an expensive hotel.

He'd overpaid her and promised the pay would remain the same as long as she cleaned it the exact same way every time.

It was an easy thing to agree to.

Now, Jasmine parked her ten-year-old Toyota Corolla in Lee's driveway, gathered her cleaning supplies, and let herself into the house with the spare key Lee had provided.

Immediately, she noticed a smell.

It was unusual and not one she had experienced before.

Immediately, she thought of her cleaning supplies and what she would have to do to make sure the odor was gone.

Henry Lee had been very clear; he'd loved the way the house smelled when she was done and she was to make sure it consistently stayed that way.

That smell, though, she thought. *What the heck was it?*

"Hello?" Jasmine called out. She was a stocky woman with dark hair and a face that rarely smiled. Henry Lee usually stayed home and she simply cleaned around him. She did ask him to leave his office, to get him away from his computers while she cleaned. It seemed like he spent nearly all of his time in that office, and it always required the most cleaning. Jasmine guessed he ordered in his meals because his kitchen appliances looked like they were never used.

"Hello?" she called out again.

But there was no answer.

Jasmine set down her buckets, broom, and mop, and went back to the storage closet near the kitchen to retrieve the vacuum. It was top-of-the-line and she often wished her other clients would splurge on cleaning equipment like Henry Lee.

She was about to fire up the vacuum when she thought she should investigate the source of the smell.

It led to the hallway, and down toward the office.

Maybe Lee had ordered in some super stinky takeout food and left it sitting for a day or two.

"Mr. Lee?" she said, stepping around the corner into his office.

She looked at the wall, where her naked employer had been nailed in place. There was dried blood running down from his hands and feet, and Jasmine thought of Jesus Christ and the crucifixion before she screamed and ran from the room.

18

Pauling saw the message from Tallon, letting her know he was heading to Australia for a very lucrative job. She checked her watch but decided to call him in the morning. For now, she tapped out a quick congratulations and told him that it worked out well; that she would be spending at least a couple of weeks in New York to see what happened with the FBI case.

For the moment, she decided not to tell him about the Reacher message written on the wall of the crime scene. She didn't know what it meant, so until she did, she would keep it to herself.

With that done, she logged into the FBI's database and began searching through all of the cases Giles had been assigned to.

As the file list populated her screen, Pauling let out a long, frustrated breath.

There were hundreds, maybe even more than a thousand. Every case he'd ever been involved with, even tangentially, was included. The number was a surprise to her, but then when she thought of how many minor items had come across her desk back then, it started to make sense. But making sense was one thing, figuring out how to actually glean anything from all of this information was another.

She had to narrow them down.

The obvious method for doing that was to cross reference Jack Reacher.

It only took her a few keystrokes and she had the answer.

0 results.

Great.

Edward Giles and Jack Reacher had never even remotely worked on a case together. At least, officially. It would have required some degree of official involvement to merit being entered into a report and thus into the database.

That criteria had clearly not been met.

So why had Giles been murdered "for Reacher"?

Pauling drummed her fingers on the desktop and considered the implications. There simply wasn't time to dig through every one of Giles' cases, even if she separated the violent from the non-violent, which was a sketchy approach to begin with. The non-violent cases could be just as much a possibility as the others. There had been plenty of innocuous investigations that had suddenly exploded in a frenzy of violence.

Cases were like people; you never really could tell which one was going to go off the deep end.

Pauling sighed.

The other way to do it would be to search the FBI database for all cases involving Reacher.

He'd often been in New York, Pauling thought. And, a little guilty, she had to admit she'd searched him before and knew that he'd been romantically linked with an attorney in the city, the daughter of an Army general.

It was definitely another best way forward.

She thought about it objectively and knew it was the right decision, but her conscience questioned if her past experience with Reacher had pushed her in that direction.

As in, a chance to get re-involved with him.

Pauling immediately thought of Tallon and pushed the past away.

No, that had nothing to do with it.

The stakes were higher than that.

All that being said, she retrieved a fresh legal pad and a pen, and dove into the FBI's history with Jack Reacher.

19

They were back on the road in the Mercedes-Benz motor home, but had only a short way to travel.

Their new destination was south of Atlanta, near Macon, Georgia.

It was far enough from Henry Lee's home, but close enough for what they needed to do next.

The team leader sent the rest of the men off to their respective hotel rooms and he stayed in the motor coach.

His name was Torrance, although his men didn't know that, and now, from a compartment next to the driver's seat, he retrieved a satellite phone equipped with the latest and most sophisticated encryption hardware.

No one would be listening, even if they desperately tried.

He dialed the number from memory.

"It's done," he said.

The man on the other end of the line offered no compliments or complaints. He simply grunted.

"Sit tight," he said and disconnected.

Torrance sat for a moment and looked at the phone.

This had never happened before. Instructions were always given immediately.

He felt something rise inside and he knew what it was.

Dread.

When things changed, it was always for the worse. Torrance hadn't smoked a cigarette in a year but suddenly, he felt the craving spring upon him like an ambushing animal.

Sit tight.

Torrance wasn't sure, but he had a vague sense of why he felt the way he did. The man on the other end of the line had told him to wait.

As in, wait...

I'm on my way.

20

Tallon finished loading his gear into his SUV and went back to the house to arm the security system. It was a process that took a fair amount of time, mainly because the system itself was fairly complex and required several steps.

Once the exterior cameras had been activated, the motion sensors engaged and the entire system armed, Tallon pressed the exit button.

It gave him sixty seconds to leave the house. A loud beep sounded every few seconds to warn him time was running out. As it got closer to the sixty-second window, the pace of the beeping increased.

He made it outside with plenty of time to spare, and once he knew the system was fully engaged, he climbed into his SUV and pulled onto the road leading to town.

It was another beautifully dry day, something of which he never tired. There had been so many wet, soggy days in bitter cold that Tallon never complained if the sun was shining. It was why he'd chosen this home, in this location.

He ran through a checklist of what he needed and double-checked in his mind that he hadn't forgotten anything. No weapons had been required for this trip, save a folding knife he would check with his luggage.

His buddy in Australia would provide all of the guns needed, as it was occasionally a pain to check a firearm. It was still legal, as long as the gun was in a hard case without ammunition.

The road was clear and Tallon found himself leaning forward in the driver's seat, anxious to get moving. There was the familiar feeling of excitement at the start of a mission. A part of him had worried about becoming "domesticated" with Pauling moving in, but he knew that was a bunch of bullshit. If anything, he'd been training more with Pauling around, especially with the weapons. She was a crack shot and they'd had a lot of fun with competitive shooting.

Tallon glanced down at the speedometer and saw he was making good time. It would take him less than an hour to reach the airport.

There were distant clouds on the edge of the horizon, and as his gaze moved out beyond the hardscrabble desert floor, he wondered about the geography of his destination. Australia was home to many varying climates and he wasn't entirely sure of what he would find when he was there.

That was part of the fun.

A certain level of surprise was enjoyable.

When there became too many unexpected discoveries, that was usually when the mission went sideways.

He was confident this wouldn't be the case. He knew the man he would be working for very well, as they'd stood shoulder-to-shoulder through some pretty vicious fighting.

No, Tallon didn't have any doubts about what lay ahead.

It was going to be a good one, he knew.

He could feel it.

21

The key, as far as Pauling was concerned, was New York. Jack Reacher. Edward Giles. The brutal murder of an FBI agent on Long Island.

Since she couldn't find any direct link between Giles and Reacher, Pauling decided to see Reacher's links not only to the FBI, but more importantly, to New York.

Starting with herself.

It was how she'd met Reacher in the first place. Edward Lane had been a notorious mercenary who claimed his wife had been kidnapped. Lane had been a player in one of Pauling's cases when she'd worked at the FBI and it was that connection that ultimately led her to Reacher.

Or, led Reacher to her.

In any event, she and Reacher had ultimately rescued Lane's wife who turned out to be running away from her husband, not a mysterious kidnapper. The final resolution had turned out to be an epic gun battle in the UK.

Pauling was able to rule out her case, as she knew for a fact that Edward Giles had absolutely nothing to do with Edward Lane, or the case Pauling had handled. In fact, she remembered clearly that he'd been assigned as a liaison working with a different government agency at that time.

Pauling felt a vague sense of relief. By eliminating the Edward Lane case, she had effectively removed herself from the current picture. There would be no need for Arnie Steele to start digging around in her past and the Edward Lane case.

It was a fact: Giles' murder had nothing to do with anything she'd been involved with alongside Jack Reacher.

The next reference to Reacher came in the files of agent Theresa Lee, a woman Pauling knew only superficially. She scanned the case – a woman's suicide that eventually involved references to the Afghanistan war. Pauling cross-referenced Giles' cases at that time and found he was investigating a racketeering case involving disputes over illegal operations in New York's harbor.

Another half-hour of fruitless searching saw no connection between Giles and Theresa Lee's case involving Reacher.

Pauling continued on for several hours, but other than minor references to cases in DC and out West, she found no other evidence with implications for the current situation.

As far as she could tell, Jack Reacher not only had never worked with Edward Giles, he'd had very little involvement with the New York office.

In other words, she was back to square one.

22

The FBI team had moved from the big conference room to a smaller one next to Steele's office. It wasn't so much that they didn't need the space as he wanted to have instant control over any developments. From his vantage point, he could see everyone coming in and out of the conference room and he could join them within seconds.

Some might label him a control freak, but Steele knew how to get the job done.

He'd had his assistant decorate one side of the room's walls with everything Giles had worked on.

On the opposite wall, he'd posted everything the FBI had on Jack Reacher.

Giles' wall was full.

Reacher's was sketchy at best.

Steele was not happy. He'd given himself the Reacher angle, figuring that's where the pay dirt would be, but so far, the well had come up dry.

He had only invited himself, Sullivan and Wyman to the current meeting.

"Sully, tell me what you have," Steele said.

Sullivan scratched at his red goatee, a tell, in Steele's opinion. Sullivan always did that when he either had no news or bad news.

"We've been over everything. As far as any bad guys Giles put away, they're all either still in prison or dead."

"Even if they're in prison, they could still order a hit," Steele pointed out.

"True, but we went through all the prison records, including the mail, visitors, messages, and there's nothing."

"It'd be a powerful act of revenge to murder an FBI agent on the eve of their retirement," Steele pointed out. "Someone who really hated him."

"Yeah, but it's not like there was a public announcement that Giles was retiring," Sullivan countered. "Hell, half the office wasn't even aware of it. How the hell would some lousy bastard out on Rikers Island know?"

Steele didn't have an answer.

"We're going to keep chasing down leads, but we've already gone back a dozen years and now we're really getting into the old stuff," Sullivan said, his voice signaling his disappointment. "The further back we go, the less likely it seems someone would still be holding such a powerful grudge."

Steele turned to Wyman.

"My net was cast pretty wide and we've got some possible leads, but none of them have to do with Giles," she said.

"Tell me about the leads you do have," Steele said.

"Do you remember Spark Plug Rostini?"

"Yeah."

"Well, he got out last week."

The image of a short, stocky Sicilian man entered Steele's mind. David Rostini, nicknamed Spark Plug, had been sent away for twenty years for armed robbery and conspiracy.

"Any connection to Giles?"

"No," Wyman answered. "But he did return to Long Island. However, he developed pretty severe diabetes and he's been writing children's books."

"You're kidding me," Sullivan said. "See Jane kill Jack?"

"What else?" Steele interrupted.

"The usual terrorist chatter Homeland Security is chasing down. A Russian mobster was killed yesterday in Brooklyn but the local cops think it was a pretty clear case of road rage. Nothing to do with their actual organized crime activities."

Steele's assistant brought in a tray of coffee in paper cups and placed it on the center of the table.

"That's it?" Steele asked Wyman.

She nodded.

"Okay, well we've got nothing so far with Reacher," Steele said. His teeth were gritted and the words came out like machine gun bullets. "We've ruled out the Edward Lane thing, and the Theresa Lee case. He's popped up here and there on some other things, but as far as New York and Giles, nothing so far."

Sullivan reached out and plucked one of the coffee cups from the tray.

"This is bullshit," he said. "Somewhere out there is the guy who murdered Giles and his wife, and we can't let him get away with it."

"We keep chasing down leads," Wyman said. "It's all we can do."

"And widen the scope," Steele said.

"How?" Sullivan replied.

The muscles along Steele's jaw twitched.

"Let me handle that."

23

T he affluent neighborhood whose key attribute of quiet serenity had attracted Henry Lee, was now anything but.

Multiple police cars ringed Lee's home, along with an ambulance and the recent addition of a crime scene van.

Yellow tape had been placed all around the house, and inside, the medical examiner was surveying the horrific scene in Henry Lee's home office.

The dead man was still nailed to the wall. Dried rivers of blood leaked from the body to the floor.

"Holy shit," one of the local cops said.

"Wait until the news jackals get a load of this," one of the other officers said.

"Let's keep that from happening as long as we can," the medical examiner said as he watched his crime scene photographer snap a close-up of the two words written on the wall in the dead man's blood.

The photographer lowered his camera and looked at the medical examiner.

"What the hell is a Reacher?" he asked.

24

P auling's eyes snapped open.

She glanced at the clock next to her bed.

Just past three in the morning.

She felt disoriented, dazed slightly from a dream about Jack Reacher and a vague memory of running through a maze of train tracks running alongside a river with the skyline of New York in the background. In the dream, Pauling had been chasing someone. But the person was much faster and was getting away, opening up more and more distance between them.

The person was a man. Very tall. Athletic, but very slim.

Who was he?

Pauling closed her eyes. This used to happen quite often when she worked at the Bureau, as her mind endlessly chewed over a case or a problem for which she couldn't find a solution. Sometimes, she wondered if her brain was working so hard as she slept that it forced her body to wake up.

Now what?

Pauling vacillated between getting up and making some coffee, or rolling over and trying to get back to sleep.

In the end, she split the difference and remained in bed, her eyes open, staring at the ceiling.

What was she missing? Why had her subconscious put her near a set of railroad tracks chasing a tall man?

Who was he?

She retreated to her last thoughts before she finally fell asleep last night. They had revolved around the Giles case, naturally. The link between Reacher and Giles. There wasn't one.

It was easy to understand the running in her dream; she was chasing down leads, confused by a lack of direction and any clear signals.

Maybe the man she was chasing was Giles' killer. But how would she know that? Why had her subconscious made him so tall and thin? Where had that come from?

The one thing she knew was that the running man wasn't Reacher.

Reacher wasn't quite that tall, and he certainly wasn't skinny. Jack Reacher was 6' 5" and somewhere in the neighborhood of 280 pounds. Massive shoulders, long arms, and a deep chest. The kind of guy who strikes fear in the hearts of weaker men.

No, the running man wasn't Reacher.

This man was a little taller, and a lot thinner. Maybe from a distance he would look like Reacher. Or like he was related to him–

Pauling sat bolt upright in bed.

Her eyes were wide and they stared into the darkness of the bedroom as her mind raced.

A relative.

Another Reacher.

She thought back to her time with Jack Reacher and remembered that he told her he had a brother.

A brother named Joe.

Joe Reacher.

25

Tallon had arrived in Pensacola, Florida, via a commercial flight, and taken a taxi to a private airport not far from the Navy base. The instructions for his travel had been sent via email and now, he looked around the small airport.

The tarmac was nearly empty.

He scanned the nearby open-air gates and saw only a single mechanic in coveralls slowly walking toward a twin-engine plane with a commercial logo on the side. Tallon had assumed someone from the operation would meet him, but if not, he would figure out which plane he was supposed to board.

The flight here had been bumpy and he'd been unable to sleep. The cab driver had been a bad one, accelerating and then slamming on the brakes. It was a monotonous back-and-forth that had made Tallon want to kick the driver out of the taxi and take over driving himself.

He had his gear by his side, and he'd been told that a military aircraft would take him from Pensacola to another military base in the Caribbean, and from there, to Australia.

But now, Tallon was confused. He'd never seen an airport, even a small private one like this, so empty.

He finally spotted the plane he was supposed to board, as he'd been given the tail number and description.

Tallon walked toward it, saw the rear door was open and stowed his gear next to it.

A man appeared at the top of the portable stairs leading to the fuselage door. He was dressed in khakis and a white shirt with a pair of pilot's wings over the breast pocket.

He smiled and waved at Tallon.

"All aboard," he called out.

Tallon glanced around him and shrugged his shoulders. He climbed the steps and saw that the cockpit door was now closed.

The rest of the plane was empty.

Was he going to be the only passenger?

It wouldn't be the first time he'd traveled solo on a flight. Many times he'd had to catch a cargo plane and been the only human cargo. Plus, this mission might be fairly secretive and by limiting the number of people involved, the better. So maybe he was the only guy from the U.S. who was going to take part.

He settled into the first seat on the aisle but decided not to buckle up. He didn't have a whole lot of confidence the flight was going to happen any time soon, and it was rare that someone would spend the money to fly one person anywhere, let alone somewhere into the Caribbean.

He settled into his seat and waited.

26

T orrance loaded the men into the motor home and drove them southeast from Macon, Georgia, into a stretch of the Piedmont national forest. It was government land, he believed, or most of it was. There was virtually no traffic and no sign of human habitation.

The terrain was rugged with steep inclines and declines and thick vegetation.

He had his hands full winding the big vehicle along a series of twisty roads until he reached an intersection. To the right was a dirt road that almost looked like a service trail.

He double-checked his instructions.

Yes, this was the turn.

He carefully maneuvered the big Benz onto the narrow path and then drove slowly forward. The sound of small stones bouncing off the bottom of the vehicle was a steady stream of percussion as they rolled forward. Occasionally, a rogue branch would scrape the side of the motor coach, like fingernails along a blackboard.

Finally, the road opened up and to the right, Torrance

spotted a 4x4 parked with its front facing forward. The windows were tinted and he couldn't see inside.

He guided the big coach off the dirt road until it was halfway into the space near the SUV and then parked.

Torrance waited until the cloud of dust he'd kicked up passed, and then he opened the motor home's doors. The two men in the back of the vehicle exited after him.

"Wait here," he told them.

It felt good to be out and walking. He was tempted to stretch but thought better of it. The man in the 4x4 was not someone to be treated casually.

Torrance walked toward the SUV, stepped up to the driver's door and knocked gently on the window. There was no reaction. Maybe the man had parked and was in the woods taking a piss–

Behind him, he heard two quick coughs that he recognized as not coming from a human being, but rather, a suppressed handgun.

He turned, and saw his two men facedown in the dirt, blood seeping from bullet holes in their heads into the dirt and gravel of the parking space.

Behind them, he saw a man with a pistol and a huge sound suppressor at the end.

"Hello, Bravo," Torrance said.

27

"Shit, you're not going to believe this," Wyman said.

She had rushed into Steele's office with a computer printout in hand.

"This better be good," Steele growled at her. He'd been on the phone with a Bureau attorney in DC, trying to gain access to classified records, so far, to no avail.

"It is," Wyman said. Her face was flushed.

Steele scanned the document.

"What the hell?" he nearly shouted, getting to his feet. He studied the paperwork in his hand, which was a detailed synopsis of the crime scene found at Henry Lee's murder. Wyman had placed an alert on anything that included references to details of the Giles case, including the word "Reacher."

The alert had popped up less than five minutes ago on her computer.

"Atlanta?" Steele shouted. "What the hell does Atlanta have to do with Giles and who the hell is Henry Lee?"

"I'm working on it," Wyman said. She was pumped with adrenaline, excited that Option C – all cases not directly involving Giles – had been under her domain, which was the reason she'd received the alert first.

"For Reacher," had clearly been described by the first responders on the scene at the murder site of one Henry Lee.

"Find out everything you can about Henry Lee. Somewhere there has to be a connection between him, Giles and Reacher. Do it now," Steele barked at her.

As Wyman left the office, she heard Steele giving urgent orders to his administrative assistant.

The gist was that Steele wanted to be on a plane to Atlanta, immediately.

28

"*Joe worked in Treasury.*"

Pauling remembered Reacher telling her those words. Officially, U.S. Department of Treasury.

Joe Reacher worked for Treasury.

Pauling bounded from her bed and practically ran to her computer. She could barely stop her hands from shaking.

Treasury.

The FBI.

Edward Giles.

Joe Reacher.

Had they ever worked together? All of her searches had been for Jack Reacher, not Joe.

Pauling double-clicked on the folder she'd created on her desktop, now full of all of the information she'd copied regarding Giles' cases. She'd focused her attention on all of his FBI cases, and had largely ignored the few times he'd been loaned out as a liaison to other government entities.

But Giles had been. The question was, had he ever been loaned to Treasury, where he might have rubbed shoulders with Joe Reacher?

She remembered noticing that during the Edward Lane case, Pauling had discovered Giles had been working as a liaison for a different government agency.

Now, she raced through the files.

In one case, Giles had been sent to Los Angeles to help organize a massive raid on an illegal immigration operation. He'd been more of a consultant on that one, tasked with helping the DEA and Homeland Security.

Pauling found another instance where Giles had briefly been transferred to a diplomatic office in Europe. Something about a threat to kill an employee of the American Embassy.

That definitely was not the one she was looking for.

Her last chance was a case Giles had been assigned to where he'd been tasked with helping a man code named "Polo."

Polo was with Treasury.

Pauling smiled.

Jack Reacher had told her that his brother Joe had been born in Palo, somewhere in the Philippine Islands.

Joe Reacher was Polo.

Pauling was sure of it.

She skimmed the details of the case and learned that "Polo" had been working on a counterfeiting case that had eventually involved Giles.

For Reacher.

Pauling shook her head.

They'd been looking for the wrong Reacher.

Bravo gestured at the dead bodies on the ground, then spoke to Torrance.

"Get rid of them, and then follow me."

He walked back to his 4x4, climbed inside and waited.

Torrance went to the back of the motor home, found a shovel and some plastic tarp and came back to the two dead men.

He rolled their bodies onto the tarp, and then dragged them off the shoulder of the road into the forest.

When he was at least fifty yards from the dirt road and totally blocked from any line of sight, he started digging the graves.

The ambush was set.

Pauling had staked out the coffee shop she knew Wyman always stopped at before work. It was just after seven in the morning and Pauling knew she had to get the information she'd discovered into the Bureau's hands, but she didn't want to just call up and offer it.

Not only would it piss off a bunch of people, it might raise far too many questions concerning how Pauling had found the information. She had no intention of drawing the focus of the FBI toward herself. Plus, she knew that if Steele suspected she was snooping around on her own, all hell would break loose.

So instead, she decided to strategically intercept her friend on neutral territory.

She'd gotten herself a large coffee for both herself and Wyman, and now she waited.

As she sipped her dark brew, Pauling considered the implications of what she'd found.

Joe Reacher and Edward Giles.

A joint task force investigating a counterfeiting operation. It was the kind of case Treasury was designed for and
the fact they'd asked the FBI for some assistance wasn't
surprising. It happened quite often, especially in the "new"
culture of law enforcement where all agencies were
supposed to work together. They'd definitely gotten better
during Pauling's tenure, but still had a ways to go.

So why now?

Why kill Giles? It had been years since that investigation
was completed, with a bevy of convictions.

The door opened and Wyman stepped in. Her eyes
seemed to immediately find Pauling who gestured she
should join her by raising the second cup of coffee.

Wyman slid onto the high stool across from her. She had
on her trademark gray steel glasses and a subdued blue
power suit. Everything about Wyman screamed this was a
woman not to be trifled with.

"Pauling, this is a pleasant surprise."

Wyman cocked an eyebrow at her indicating she knew
this was no accident.

"Yes, but we have to talk fast," Pauling said. "I know you
don't want to be late for work and I don't want to risk anyone
else from the office spotting us."

Wyman sipped her coffee and waited.

"The Reacher you're looking for is *not* Jack Reacher. It's
Joe Reacher. Jack's brother. Joe worked for the Treasury
Department and the last case he worked on, Giles had been
assigned afterward as a liaison."

Wyman's jaw popped open slightly.

"Jesus, Pauling, how did you find this out?" She looked
around the coffee shop as if someone from the Bureau
might be listening.

"A little insider knowledge and a fair amount of detective work."

"How did I miss that?" Pauling could tell that Wyman took it personally she hadn't discovered the link. As if she were still the student and Pauling the master.

"Joe Reacher was using a code name for most of the operation. Polo. It's probably why his name never appeared."

Wyman shook her head. "Unbelievable."

"There's more," Pauling said.

"Of course there is, you are always full of surprises, Lauren Pauling."

"Jack Reacher actually was involved in that case, too, but there won't be any mention of him, either."

"Why not?"

"He's a bit of a ghost. He covers his tracks well and then usually slips out of town unnoticed. I'm pretty sure that's what happened here."

"How can you be sure?"

"Because Joe Reacher was murdered during that investigation. And Jack told me he found out who had killed him, and made them pay."

"Pay? As in he arrested them?"

"No."

Wyman blinked and then she understood.

"Oh."

Pauling got to her feet.

"One last question," Wyman said. "Where was this counterfeiting operation going on? Here in New York? DC?"

"No. In a place called Margrave, Georgia. Just outside of Atlanta."

Wyman's jaw popped open again. She pointed at Pauling's chair, indicating she should sit back down.

"Hold on, Pauling, now it's my turn for a surprise."

31

T allon heard the plane's engines come to life at the same time he heard footsteps on the ladder leading to the fuselage door.

"Hey," a man said as he clambered on board. He was dressed in civilian clothes, but had a military presence about him.

Tallon nodded back to him.

At the rear of the plane, the hatch door opened and someone began loading luggage into the rear bay.

Tallon was glad to see signs of life other than himself. He'd wondered if there'd been a logistical mistake and he was on the wrong plane. He checked his Ball NEDU watch and saw they were at least on schedule.

But now that there was someone else, he felt a little better. There was something about flying on a plane as the only passenger that was off-putting. He'd done it before and there was always the feeling someone would forget there was a person on board. A bit irrational, perhaps, but always a possibility.

With the complete lack of other aircraft activity, he

figured once the bags were loaded and the pilot ready to go, they would take off pretty soon–

He had the briefest sensation of metal on the skin of his neck and then 50,000 volts shot through his body.

Tallon was tackled to the floor by the man who'd just gotten on board.

Tallon struggled but the man was now on top of him. A second man, from the back of the plane who'd been pretending to load the luggage, joined in.

Finally, the cockpit door opened and the pilot stepped out, a set of plastic zip ties in his hand.

The engines had been shut off.

Tallon's face was pushed into the floor of the plane and he felt himself jerking and twitching, unable to move as his arms were pinned behind him. He closed his eyes and cursed himself.

Stupid, he thought. He remembered thinking earlier that maybe he'd gotten too comfortable with Pauling. Like he'd lost his edge.

Well, he'd ignored his intuition and now he was paying for it.

As if to confirm his bleak self-assessment, a cloth with chloroform was slapped over Tallon's face.

And then all he saw was darkness.

32

W yman carried the stack of files and went directly to Director Tisdale's office. She was met by a secretary who stopped her.

"It's urgent I meet with him. It has to do with Agent Giles' murder and the Director will definitely want to see this right away."

Tisdale's secretary went to the office, opened the door and peeked her head inside. She stepped back, and motioned for Wyman to enter.

She did so, and found Tisdale seated behind his desk in the process of hanging up his phone.

"Agent Wyman," he said, in his reserved voice.

"Sir, I found a connection between Reacher and Giles, but Agent Steele is en route to Atlanta and I wanted to share it with you immediately."

Tisdale glanced at the folders in her hand and then said, "Proceed."

She put the folders on his desk and walked him through what she had learned after having been tipped off from Pauling.

The counterfeiting operation had taken Joe Reacher's life, as well as many others, including a dirty FBI agent by the name of Picard. By the time Giles was involved, the case was nearly closed.

All that had been left was for Giles to put the original informant, a man named Paul Hubble, into witness protection.

"Where was Hubble placed?" Tisdale asked.

"I don't know, sir, I'm working on that."

Tisdale made a steeple of his fingers and peered over them at Wyman.

"I understand the connection, but how does this affect our search for Giles' killer?"

Wyatt proceeded cautiously. "I'm working on that as well, sir. But the guilty party in the counterfeiting operation was a local Georgia family named Kliner. They were working with an operation in Venezuela, washing dollar bills and reprinting them as one-hundred dollar bills. Eventually, with the help of local police in Margrave, Georgia, the whole thing collapsed. The warehouses with all the money were burned to the ground."

"I see."

"However, one of the Kliners who survived, a cousin, was released from prison less than three weeks ago. Thomas Kliner. He was only eighteen at the time of the original case and had been working as a driver, nothing more."

"So you think he was seeking revenge for his family? Seems a bit extreme, doesn't it?"

Wyman had to agree.

"I'll keep looking, sir."

"Do that," Tisdale replied. "Be sure to fill in Steele and keep me up to speed."

Wyman gathered up the folders and left Tisdale's office.

She had a lot to do and wondered when Steele's plane would be landing.

33

"I *need you. Come to Margrave, Georgia. Now!*"

Pauling looked at the message and read it again, even though she'd done so twice already.

It was from Tallon.

Come to Margrave, Georgia?

Pauling tapped out a reply.

"Why?" she asked. "I thought you were heading to Australia?"

There was no response.

She tried to call the number but it went straight to voice-mail. All of Pauling's warning signals kicked into high alert. This wasn't right. Tallon had nothing to do with Joe Reacher, Edward Giles or a counterfeiting operation that had taken place years earlier.

Had someone hacked his phone? Or worse?

She doubted it, but the message made no sense.

Margrave, Georgia, was the location of the counterfeiting case where Joe Reacher had been murdered.

What the hell did it have to do with Tallon? How was he involved?

Pauling waited, but there was still no response.

Deep within her, she knew there wasn't going to be one. Whoever had killed Giles and murdered that poor man Henry Lee outside Atlanta had struck again.

They had Michael Tallon.

34

S teele waited until he'd taken in the horrors of the Henry Lee crime scene before he listened to the message from Wyman.

What he'd seen inside the house outside of Buckhead, Georgia, corroborated his suspicions. It was no copycat crime. It was the same group of killers who had butchered Edward Giles and his wife.

No doubt about it.

Unfortunately, he was left with more questions than answers. How had Henry Lee been connected with Giles or Jack Reacher?

He'd barely had time to contemplate the possible answers before Wyman's message got to him. She had sent emails containing files to prove her point, but Steele wasn't in a position to look at them on his laptop.

So he called her.

"Walk me through it," he said.

Steele listened as Wyman explained the Joe Reacher connection, his role at Treasury, and Giles' work with him on the counterfeiting organization in Margrave, Georgia.

"How did you figure this out?" he asked her.

There was only the briefest of hesitations before Wyman explained her deep dive into Giles' efforts outside the FBI, when he acted as a liaison with other departments.

Steele wasn't so sure.

He knew Wyman and Lauren Pauling had been supportive of each other's careers and wondered if Wyman had gotten some assistance from her former mentor.

Well, it didn't matter.

They had attracted a local crowd outside of Henry Lee's home, despite the local police's best efforts to keep everyone away. By now, a local news truck was set up half a block away.

It was time for Steele to bail on the scene. The local Atlanta FBI office had assigned him an agent to help assist in the investigation. He was waiting by an unmarked Bureau car, a four-door Ford with black painted wheels and an obvious antenna along with government plates. If the local news was any good, they would know this was more than just a garden-variety crime.

Steele walked up to the younger agent.

"We need to go to Margrave, Georgia. Right now."

Steele got into the front passenger seat, dug out his laptop and connected to the Internet via his mobile hotspot.

With great interest, he read the files Wyman had sent him.

35

Pauling had to marvel over Jack Reacher's ability to fade into the background. She'd had plenty of time on the flight from New York to Atlanta to ponder how he'd managed it.

He had no doubt avenged his brother's death, helped to bring down a massive counterfeiting operation, and had then faded into the background. Probably hitchhiked or took a bus off into the distance.

It was really unbelievable.

The plane touched down and she headed to the rental car company, requesting the best sports car they had. She needed to make good time and wasn't about to push a four-cylinder subcompact to its limits.

They had a BMW 7 series with a powerful V-8 engine.

Perfect.

The drive took no time and soon she was driving the BMW through the outskirts of tiny Margrave, Georgia.

Once again, her thoughts turned to Reacher. She had no trouble imagining him taking over a town like this. She passed a small restaurant called Eno's Diner and figured Reacher had partaken in his usual breakfast of coffee, bacon and pancakes. Probably several times.

She remembered that he'd mentioned something about a blues singer being from the small town, and that was the reason for his visit.

Blind Blake or something like that.

It was classic Reacher. He'd just wandered into the small town because he'd been curious about a forgotten blues musician and had gotten into a lot more than he'd bargained for.

Pauling didn't feel any type of kismet with Reacher. He hitchhiked, drifted. Her plane ticket had been a first-class flight and now she was driving a car worth seventy thousand dollars.

She and Reacher had been so different but somehow, they had meshed.

Pauling passed the quaint little downtown, the old-fashioned barber shop and headed straight for the police station.

It would be the fastest way to possibly figure out what the hell was going on.

She pulled the BMW into a visitor parking space and went inside.

Pauling explained who she was to the cop manning the reception desk and the chief of police came out to see her. His name was Barkin and after he'd looked her over, made sure she wasn't a loon just in off the street, escorted her back to his office.

"The Kliner case," she said as she settled into a chair across from his desk.

Barkin let out a low whistle. He was a middle-aged man with a bushy moustache and a tired expression, but his blue eyes were sharp and focused. The office smelled vaguely of coffee and pipe tobacco.

"What a nightmare," he said. "When that whole thing went down, the entire town almost went with it. That illegal money had been supporting everyone and everything for years. The Kliners had paid off pretty much all the merchants in Margrave. They got something like a couple grand a week just to keep quiet. People took the money. Can you blame them?"

"So what happened?"

"Well, once the money stopped it was almost like what they call a market correction, in economical terms. Quite a few businesses went under, and half the town left. But slowly, things turned around and now the town is doing fine. While it's not booming like before, at least it's real. We had a good-sized company that makes commercial refrigerators set up shop just outside of town. A factory that employs about a hundred local people. It's a start."

"What about the detective in charge of the Kliner case? Is he still around?"

"Finlay? He retired. Moved out to California."

"Officer Roscoe?" She'd been a local cop key in the eventual cracking of the Kliner case, according to Wyman.

"She married, moved up to Charlotte. Has three kids now."

Pauling nodded.

"Paul Hubble?" Hubble had been the leaker; he'd contacted the Treasury Department and essentially gotten Joe Reacher killed. From what Pauling had been able to figure out from the case file, he'd gone into witness protection.

"No sign of him."

"Has anything changed recently? Any news on the Kliner front?"

For the first time, Barkin's expression faltered. He hesitated.

"Just a rumor," he began.

Pauling waited.

"Word is a Kliner cousin, name of Thomas, tasted freedom for the first time in a number of years. No idea where he went, though. Haven't seen him around here. No reason to come back, anyway. Everyone's long gone."

"Yeah," she said.

Pauling knew he was wrong.

And she suspected that he did, too.

36

T allon opened his eyes and immediately sensed movement.

He was in a vehicle. Not an airplane or a car.

Some kind of van, or motor home. He was hog-tied and his arms were locked around a steel stanchion bolted to the floor of the vehicle.

He tried to glance around, but he couldn't move his shoulders enough to turn and his back was to the front of the vehicle.

Tallon silently cursed himself.

Sloppy, he thought. Just plain amateurish to let himself get jumped like that. He was angry and embarrassed.

The plastic ties were cutting into his wrist and all he could see was the dark reflection of highway lines passing by. He had a headache from the chloroform and his neck ached from where the Taser had blasted him.

So stupid, he thought. Clearly, his buddy's email had been hacked. That actually should have tipped him off; the fact that he'd never actually had a phone conversation with him. It had all taken place over email. Tallon wondered what would have happened had he called. The call probably would have been intercepted or they'd have let it go to voicemail and then responded with an email.

His buddy in Australia probably had no idea that Tallon thought he was en route.

Okay, enough bitching, he thought. Time to take action. He always felt better when he was doing something and the way to make himself come to terms with the fact that he'd been abducted?

Turn the tables.

Now.

He glanced down and saw that his captors hadn't taken the shoelaces from his boots. He smiled, but at the same time it pissed him off. It made him angry because their failure to do so was a sign of their lack of professionalism. Which made the fact they'd nabbed him sting all the more.

Well, he was about to make them wish they'd never laid a hand on him.

Without shifting his body and as subtly as possible, he slid his hands down toward his boots.

37

Pauling left the Margrave Police station and drove down to Eno's Diner. She took a booth at the back of the place and ordered coffee and a turkey sandwich.

The place was empty save for a young couple who looked like they had just graduated high school. A waitress was washing glasses behind the counter and in the back, a cook was making something on the grill. She could hear the sizzling and assumed it was either sausage or bacon. Or both.

Pauling drank her coffee and contemplated the vagaries of human nature. Over the years, she'd come to recognize that the origins of most criminal activity could be traced back to three of the most basic of human desires.

Lust.

Greed.

Hate.

Ninety-nine times out of a hundred, most of her cases had come down to one of those primary motivations.

Of the three, greed was the clear frontrunner. One way

or the other, it was usually about the money. America was a capitalist society. It required money to survive. If you didn't have money, you weren't going to make it. Period. Compared to that, lust and hate seemed almost frivolous.

She suspected greed played the key role in the murder of Giles. The case had led back to a counterfeiting operation, and what was a better example of greed than producing fake money?

The question was, what were the killers after?

It sounded like the money had gone up in flames.

But what if it hadn't? Or at least not all of it?

At the height of the Kliner operation, hundreds upon hundreds of millions of dollars were in play.

So what if there had been a warehouse no one knew about? Or a late delivery that never got a chance to dump its load into what would become a terribly expensive bonfire?

How much would that have been? Five million? Ten? Fifty?

Pauling thought back to what Wyman had told her about the murder in Buckhead. Henry Lee. A financial advisor. A wizard with numbers who served a select clientele.

He hadn't been mentioned in any of the Kliner case files.

Pauling slammed down her coffee cup so loudly the couple in the booth ahead of her turned and looked.

Henry Lee hadn't been involved.

But Pauling was suddenly sure of one thing.

One of his clients almost certainly had.

38

Plastic zip ties are a thing of beauty. Cheap. Ubiquitous and strong as hell.

The only downside?

Susceptible to friction. Heating plastic makes it weak, plain and simple.

Friction was exactly what Michael Tallon was applying via the shoe lace in his hands. He'd unthreaded it from his right boot and was now sawing it back and forth against the zip ties holding his hands together. It was awkward as hell, especially as his hands were still circling the steel stanchion.

It was taking him longer than he liked because he was doing it in a way that showed no movement of his body. He didn't want the men at the front of the vehicle to notice anything about him. He couldn't see them, had no idea how closely they were watching him. Did they even know the chloroform had worn off? Or did they assume he was still unconscious.

He desperately hoped it was the latter.

Within five minutes, the zip ties snapped apart and

Tallon twitched, just slightly. The sudden jolt of release had come too quickly and he hadn't been able to control his body from registering the sensation.

He hoped they hadn't noticed.

Behind him, he heard one of the men snoring. That meant one was driving, and the other one was doing what?

Watching him?

He hoped not.

Unfortunately, Tallon heard the rustle of fabric and then the soft footfalls of somebody walking on carpet.

"You awake, shithead?" the voice said.

The man must have seen Tallon's slight movement.

Tallon felt cold steel press against his neck. This time, it wasn't a Taser. It was the muzzle of a pistol.

He felt the vehicle slow and raised his head. He couldn't see behind him, only sensed the vague shape of a man standing over his left shoulder.

Pulling his arms against the stanchion, he jerked as if the zip ties were holding him strong, then twisted to get a better look at his captor, and show him that he was still secure.

Lull him into being overconfident.

The gun had moved back several inches and the vehicle came to a complete stop. The man with the gun glanced back toward the driver, who was now getting to his feet.

Tallon's hands, now free, shot up. One grabbed the gun, the other the man's fingers which he squeezed until he heard bones breaking.

The gun came free and Tallon rotated his grip until the butt of the gun was in his palm and then he shot directly upward, catching the man above him in the bottom, meaty part of the jaw, the bullet crashing upward through his brain and splattering blood and gristle onto the ceiling of the motor coach.

The driver had just enough time to start a move toward the passenger seat, where Tallon assumed he had a gun.

Tallon shot him twice in the chest and the driver's momentum carried him into the foot well, where he fell to the floor, his feet sticking up near the steering wheel.

The snoring man had jerked awake and he now had a panicked expression on his face, but he also had a gun in his hand. He was getting his bearings, trying to figure out which way to shoot.

Tallon would have liked to interrogate him, but instead, he had to shoot him in the head, just above his ear.

He toppled over into nearly the exact same position in which he'd been sleeping.

Tallon got to his feet, shook off the remains of the zip ties, and threaded his shoelace back into his boot, lacing it tightly.

He studied the dead men. They looked absolutely ordinary. All three were white, possibly ex-military, but certainly not elite. Low-level hired thugs, nothing more.

From the pockets of each man he dug out a wallet and a cell phone. He took all three wallets and all three cell phones and shoved them into his pockets, and then did a quick survey of the inside of the motor home.

He saw weapons including guns and knives, as well as cutting tools and plenty of plastic tarps.

A killing crew.

He remembered the autopsy Pauling had showed him. No doubt these guys were the ones who'd butchered the FBI agent in New York. Tallon had spotted the nail gun in the motor home.

Tallon glanced out the window and saw they had stopped at a truck stop.

Perfect.

He was hungry.

He would eat, and try to figure out who the hell had targeted him.

And why.

"Wyman."

Pauling spoke quietly into the phone.

She was still at Eno's Diner and knew that calling Wyman directly was a risky move, but Pauling felt like time was of the essence. Plus, she knew that by talking to the Chief of Police of Margrave that sooner or later word would get back to Steele, if it hadn't already.

"Have you had a chance to look at Henry Lee's clients?" Pauling asked. She was operating under the assumption that someone somewhere had managed to squirrel away a sizeable chunk of the counterfeit cash. That person would most likely have been Paul Hubble. And since Henry Lee managed money for wealthy clients, the only link she could think of was Hubble. The question is, could she determine who, and where, Hubble was?

"Doing that right now," Wyman said. Pauling could hear the tapping of keys on a computer.

"He only had a dozen active clients," Wyman told her. "But each one was very wealthy. Smallest portfolio is worth twelve million."

"Huh. Anything jump out at you?"

"No. Seven of them are overseas. One is Canadian. The other lives in Argentina."

Pauling thought about the implications. She supposed the people behind the murders could be managing the operation from outside the United Sates, but she doubted it. Certainly, they would have their people in place stateside to manage any emergencies.

Still, it didn't seem likely.

This was an American crime, on American soil with the murders in New York and Atlanta. Plus, the original case had taken place in Georgia, although part of the counterfeiting operation had been located in Venezuela.

"Any in Venezuela?" Pauling asked.

"No."

"That leaves three Americans?"

"Correct."

"One lives in Malibu," Wyman said. "The other lives in Seattle, I think he's a software guy, the name seems familiar but I could be imagining it. The third has an address in Montana."

"Any major shifts in their funds? Big withdrawals? Lots of activity?"

"None that I can see, but there's a fair amount of information here and I'm not a financial investigator." Pauling knew the FBI had a whole department full of people who dealt only with white-collar financial crimes. They could look at spreadsheets and know instantly when something smelled badly.

"Criminal history?"

"None that I can find. I ran the names, they all came back clean."

Pauling chewed her lip.

"What are the names?" she asked.

Wyman read them off. "Darnell Poutrie. Steve Kozmos. John McCartney."

The names rattled around in Pauling's head.

The young couple in the booth across from her paid their bill and left. She was alone in the diner. The waitress cleared the young couple's plates and wiped off the table, glanced at Pauling's coffee cup and Pauling gave her the signal she didn't need any more.

"Pauling, are you there?" Wyman asked.

She was imagining Reacher eating here. If he were here now, she could ask him his opinion. He had so much experience as an investigator, and it was the kind of experience that was very different from hers. Although he could be a man of few words, he'd shared some of his more interesting stories with her. One in particular came to mind–

Suddenly she sat up straight.

"What was the last one?"

"John McCartney."

Pauling could picture Reacher's face. The time he told her a story. *Something about a guy he'd known who was a Beatles fan. Whenever he needed an alias, the man always used a combination of the names from the band. You know, Paul Lennon. George Starr–*"

"It's John McCartney," Pauling practically shouted. "John McCartney is Paul Hubble."

40

As bad as the truck stop food looked, it tasted even worse. But Tallon was starving and he shoveled the cheeseburger into his mouth, along with a greasy pile of American fries mixed with onions and cheese, and chased it all down with black coffee and a piece of apple pie. It filled his stomach but he was vaguely worried he would feel sick in about an hour.

From his vantage point, he could see the Mercedes-Benz motor home parked along the outer edge of the lot. To its right were several big rigs. So far, no one had approached the vehicle. Tallon hoped whoever was in charge of the operation would stop by and see what had happened to his men.

Which reminded him - the drivers licenses of the three dead men meant nothing to him, mainly because they were fake. All three of them. They were Florida licenses, which meant nothing.

The phones were useless, too. Just burners with calls only made between them. The contact list was empty, save for each of the other phones.

Tallon set the wallets and two of the phones on his tray, and then carried it all over to a giant wastebasket and slid everything into the garbage, where it would no doubt soon be smothered in leftover gravy and soggy French fries.

He returned to his booth and accepted a refill on coffee.

Tallon glanced outside at the motor home. Still no activity.

He considered his options, and what his location meant. On the way into the truck stop, he'd spotted a giant road map behind Plexiglas with the "you are here" arrow, no doubt installed years ago before everyone had smartphones with electronic maps installed.

Tallon had stopped and looked at the map, registering mild surprise.

Now, he looked at the single burner phone he hadn't dumped into the trash and opened it up. He tapped out a text message to Pauling.

"It's Tallon. Right now I'm sitting in a truck stop near Margrave, Georgia," he wrote. "Where are you?"

41

B ravo cruised past the truck stop where he saw the motor home parked but continued driving down the road.

He already knew his men were dead. He'd watched from a distance as Tallon had emerged from the motor home alone.

Bravo hadn't been surprised at all. Because it was part of the plan.

It had effectively eliminated the rest of the team, so it was just Bravo and his partner, plus, it drew Tallon into the case. A chip they could play later when they needed it.

He took the on ramp to the freeway and gunned his way into the fast lane. He wouldn't go too far over the speed limit as he had no need to interact with a cop at the moment, but he also wasn't going to drive leisurely.

The flat Georgia land held no interest for him, and he pressed onward. Bravo was pleased Tallon had eliminated the crew, and saved him doing the job himself. Plus, the Feds would no doubt be able to tie evidence to the crime scenes in New York and Atlanta, temporarily satisfying them and keeping their focus here, right where they wanted it.

Bravo knew they were getting very close to the end, and that the finish line was finally in sight.

It was only a matter of time before he got what he'd been waiting for all those years, what he so rightly deserved.

He nudged the 4x4's speed up a little higher. He was getting excited and his reservoir of patience was starting to run dry.

He sped past Margrave, toward Atlanta and the airport.

42

S teele was exceptionally frustrated.

He'd talked to the chief of police and found out that a woman matching Pauling's description had been there ahead of him.

It pissed him off for several reasons. One, the stupid local cop had nothing to offer. No news of anything happening. He offered no insight on the crimes or on the past counterfeiting case. Plus, Steele sensed the police chief had an attitude.

Lastly, Steele felt that Pauling was once again one step ahead of him. It reminded him of when they'd worked together at the Bureau, as competitors. At that time, Pauling always seemed to gain the upper hand. She was smoother, smarter, and in some cases, more aggressive.

She'd put Steele in his place many times. So much so that he had often reverted to tactics that hit below the belt. At the time, he was desperate. His career was everything and he figured that the ends justified the means. Now, many years later, he realized that he had crossed the line with Pauling. He'd actively sabotaged a couple of her investigations and when he could, assigned her blame she didn't deserve and diverted credit that she had earned away from her.

Steele shook his head, chastising himself. This wasn't about Pauling. This was about Giles. And now Henry Lee. He'd studied the cases Wyman had sent him and knew they had to find the link that tied it all together. It was up to him to do it.

He'd decided to check into the only hotel in Margrave in order to study the files and set up a game plan. Now, he realized the answer was going to be back in Atlanta, or that he would need to return to New York and put a full-court press on the team.

This was his case, and he was determined to win.

There was a knock on the door and he approached to look through the keyhole. It was probably going to be the local Atlanta FBI agent, wanting to see if he'd had dinner. Or maybe grab some drinks before they returned to the city.

Steele's hand went to the pistol on his hip, just in case. The images of Giles and his wife nailed to their living room wall were still very fresh in his mind.

Steele recognized the face peering back at him from the hallway and tried to hide the shock.

He opened the door and stepped aside.

"What are you doing down here?" he asked.

His visitor raised a pistol and shot Steele in the face.

auling gasped when she read the text message on her phone. She quickly paid her bill, fired up her rented BMW and drove to where Tallon said he was waiting. It was a truck stop less than a mile from Eno's Diner.

She pulled into the parking lot of the truck stop and watched Tallon lope out of the restaurant and climb into her BMW. He had a big grin on his face.

"Hey, nice rental," he said as they quickly kissed. Pauling gunned the car out of the parking lot.

"Okay, I want you to start from the beginning," she said, still unable to grasp that Michael Tallon had somehow ended up in little Margrave, Georgia, at the same time she had. Pauling wasn't a big believer in coincidences and had already begun to suspect that someone had orchestrated the meeting.

Tallon walked her through the story, including his abduction at the military airport, and the three men he'd killed in the motor home.

"And yes," he said. "I destroyed any evidence of my presence in that motor home."

"Don't worry about it," Pauling replied. "The cops will find traces of stuff linking them to the murder of Giles and Henry Lee, no doubt."

He looked at her and she realized it was her turn to fill him in.

"Okay, now you," Tallon said.

Pauling went over the details starting from after Giles' murder and her subsequent discoveries.

Tallon followed along. "Do you get the sense someone is trying to steer the investigation a certain way?"

"Absolutely," she said. "The 'For Reacher' message was clearly designed to either explain what they were doing, or to send the Bureau in an obvious direction. And obviously, you being grabbed and driven here was another blatant move. They want us working together for some reason."

"Yeah, but who? And what are we looking for?"

"I'm looking for the person responsible for murdering the Gileses."

"And you think Paul Hubble might have the answer?"

"Or he might be the answer."

Tallon put on his seat belt as Pauling gunned the BMW onto the freeway. Very quickly they were doing well over ninety miles per hour, heading north.

"Are we going to the airport?" Tallon asked. "Catching a flight to Montana?"

"Damn right we are," Pauling answered.

44

Paul Hubble, now called John McCartney by his friends and neighbors, heard the doorbell ring.

Years earlier, he used to panic when someone showed up at his home unannounced. In his imagination, it was always one of the Kliner men, with a nail gun and plastic boots, ready to nail him to the wall, along with his family. They would cut off his genitals and do unimaginable things to his wife and daughters.

Over the years, though, that fear had passed.

Thanks mainly to repetition. As visitors came and went, Hubble gradually began to realize that the Kliners were gone, and no one but mail deliveries, neighbors and his daughters' friends would be showing up at his door.

So now, as he made his way to the front door, he figured maybe his wife had ordered something from Amazon again. Maybe that new blender she had shown him on her laptop.

It was a long walk to the front door because it was a big house. On the outskirts of Billings, it was a six-bedroom, five thousand square foot home with a gourmet kitchen, a swimming pool and a four-car garage. In that garage was one of

Hubble's most prized possessions; a Rolls-Royce Phantom. He'd upgraded from the old Bentley he used to drive.

Hubble opened the door and saw a man standing before him. Hubble didn't recognize him. He was an older gentleman, well-dressed in a suit, with neatly trimmed silver hair.

Behind him, a younger man stood, peering intently at Hubble.

The young man looked vaguely familiar to Hubble.

He had the kind of face that–

"Oh no," he said.

A Kliner.

The man in front produced a pistol from inside his suit coat. He smiled, revealing perfect teeth.

"It took me a long time to find you, Paul," he said. His voice was soft, his diction cultured and precise.

Hubble backed up and the Kliner kid shut the door behind him.

"Who are you?" Hubble asked.

"Call your family, Paul," the man said.

Hubble hesitated and the man continued. "Paul, let me be very clear. One way or the other, you're going to tell me where the money is."

Hubble heard his youngest daughter come into the kitchen from the back door.

The man's gaze never left Hubble's face. "The only thing that isn't certain is how many of your kids I'll have to kill first."

45

The rental car agency at the airport in Billings, Montana, didn't have a BMW, but it did have a Ford Mustang. Pauling rented it and opened it up on the freeway to the point where Tallon was worried they'd get arrested before they could get to the address Wyman had given Pauling that they all hoped would turn out to be Paul Hubble's residence, as provided by the witness protection program.

It took them thirty minutes to find the house in a prestigious neighborhood full of big homes spread out on multiple-acre lots. The land was quite different from Georgia's – big sweeping valley and rolling hills.

Pauling pulled up in front of the house and glanced at her phone.

"Just got a message from Wyman. Steele isn't answering his phone. No one's heard from him and they can't get in touch."

Tallon was looking at a big black SUV parked in the driveway.

"That's not Hubble's style," he said. "Didn't you say he used to drive a Bentley?"

"Maybe that's part of his new identity," Pauling replied.

"Yeah, but people can't change their personality. I highly doubt he's driving that. So either his handler is telling him to drive that thing or–"

"Or someone beat us here," Pauling said, finishing his thought.

Tallon retrieved the hard-sided case he'd used to check the two pistols he'd taken from the dead men on the motor home. He loaded both and handed one to Pauling.

"I think Hubble has company."

46

"It's in a storage unit at the edge of town. I'll take you there," Hubble said. He was crying. His wife and daughters were assembled behind him.

"Of course," the older man said. "Bring the key and we'll take her as insurance."

The man pointed at Hubble's youngest daughter. A girl of twelve with blonde hair and blue eyes.

"No, take me," Hubble's wife said.

The man raised his gun at the girl.

"I can kill her now if you'd like."

"No!" Hubble said. "Let's go. I'll take you there, no problem."

The Kliner kid stepped forward.

"Yes, you will," he said. He clubbed Hubble with the butt of his gun and Hubble sank to the floor. The young girls shrieked and Hubble's wife covered her mouth with her hands.

Kliner kicked Hubble in the ribs.

"Get up, you piece of shit," he said. "I'll teach you not to rob from my family."

The older man put his hand on Kliner's shoulder.

"Plenty of time for that later," he said. "Let's get what we came for first."

47

Pauling was nearly frozen.

She and Tallon had circled behind the house, and entered through the kitchen door.

Pauling had risked a look around the corner of the doorway leading into the kitchen and saw something she couldn't believe.

The Director of the New York FBI Office, William Tisdale, was pointing a gun at a very young girl.

Pauling ducked back from the doorway and looked at Tallon. She was shaken to the core. Tisdale? He'd ordered the murder of one of his own agents? And led everyone on a chase to find Paul Hubble?

It didn't make sense.

"What's wrong?" Tallon whispered in her ear.

"Nothing."

They heard a smack and then a body hitting the floor, followed by the screams of Hubble's kids.

Pauling decided she couldn't wait any longer.

"Let's go," she said.

She and Tallon stepped out from the kitchen, separating themselves quickly to present a wider target area.

"Drop the gun, Tisdale," Pauling said. "It's over. I've been in touch with Wyman and everyone knows you're behind this."

No one moved.

On the floor, a chubby man wearing an expensive, gold Rolex looked at her. She recognized him.

Paul Hubble.

The man standing over Hubble was tall and lanky, but his face bore faint similarities to the mug shots of the Kliner family behind the counterfeiting scheme.

Pauling knew Tallon was focused on the Kliner kid because he was directly opposite him, and her responsibility was Tisdale.

"Pauling," Tisdale said. His eyes shifted rapidly back and forth. "You always were very bright," he said.

"Why?" Pauling asked.

"Do you really think I'm the type to discuss my motivation?" he asked. "Really, Pauling, you disappoint–"

Hubble groaned and the Kliner kid moved.

He started to raise his pistol, which he'd used to club Hubble, but shifting his grip caused the slightest delay and it was all the time Tallon needed.

He fired twice. The shots were so fast they nearly blended into one sound. The bullets tore into Kliner's chest, over his heart and his arm stopped halfway up. He staggered backward and fell, his head cracking on the tile floor, his gun skittering across the room before banging into the wooden base molding.

Tisdale hadn't moved.

Pauling hadn't either, and now Tallon's pistol, along with hers, were both pointing directly at Tisdale.

"Put down the gun," Pauling said to Tisdale. "You are out of options."

The head of the FBI's New York office smiled and gave a soft laugh.

"Not quite," he said. He put the muzzle of his pistol into the soft flesh below his chin and fired upward. Blood and brains splattered onto the beveled glass sidelights of the house's front door.

Tisdale dropped to the floor amid screams and cries from Hubble's family.

Paul Hubble looked at the dead Kliner kid, and then the lifeless form of Tisdale before turning back to Pauling and Tallon.

"Jesus Christ," he said. "Who the hell are you guys?"

EPILOGUE

"You two are so cute together," Wyman said.

Tallon had grilled some filet mignon and they were now working on their second bottle of cabernet. Pauling's apartment smelled like a gourmet restaurant and she was happy to be entertaining. She and Tallon had invited Wyman over for dinner to discuss the fallout from what the Bureau was now calling the Tisdale Disaster.

Pauling laughed at Wyman's comment and she put a hand on Tallon's shoulder. She didn't know if they were cute together, but everything with Tallon just felt right.

"The whole thing was designed to smoke out Paul Hubble's true identity," Wyman said.

"Unbelievable," Tallon said. "Tisdale was head of the New York Bureau and he couldn't ferret that out?"

Wyman shook her head. "No, and believe me, he tried. But Hubble's new identity was set up by Treasury, and Tisdale couldn't get the information. Some people think he was pissed off that Giles, who'd been the liaison on that case, couldn't find out, either."

"Yeah, witness protection is a whole different ballgame," Pauling said. "A completely separate unit, highly secretive."

"Our internal affairs team dug into Tisdale's affairs and found he was broke. His wife had left him and he was trying to get enough money to try to win her back. That whole uber-composed personality he put on display? It was all a very good act, because inside he was crazed and panicked."

"So he killed Giles and planted the Reacher clue," Tallon said. "Knowing it would eventually lead back to Margrave, Georgia, and the counterfeiting scheme. Which would then give him a reason to try to blow the whole case back out into the open."

"And eventually, Paul Hubble's true identity would come out," Pauling said. "That was the plan. And somehow, he found out my history with Reacher so he made sure to get me involved, and you," she said to Tallon. "I think you were insurance that if I didn't go along and do my job as investigator well enough, he could use you as bait. Or maybe a threat."

"But how did he know that not all the money had been destroyed?" Tallon asked.

"Basic math," Wyman replied. "He'd read the reports and sure enough, the Venezuelan arm of the Kliner's operation had sent over $700 million to the Kliners in Georgia, but only $590 million had been checked into the Kliner's warehouse. Which meant that $110 million was floating around somewhere, and Tisdale guessed accurately that Hubble, the currency guy in the operation, had somehow stashed it and was dipping into it when he needed. Unbeknownst to his witness protection handlers."

"I'm still fuzzy on Henry Lee's role in this, though," Pauling said.

"Chalk that one up to Steele," Wyman said. "God rest his soul."

Pauling, despite their differences over the years, had been shocked and saddened to learn that Tisdale had killed Steele back in Georgia.

"Steele discovered Lee?"

"Inadvertently," Wyman said. "When he cast his net for Giles' old cases, Henry Lee's name had come up. It seems that Treasury had looked at Lee's books, Tisdale was monitoring Steele's progress. When he saw that a guy who handled money for uber-wealthy clients less than an hour from Margrave had been looked at, Tisdale rolled the dice."

Wyman's glass was empty and Tallon refilled it.

"Lust, greed and hate," Pauling said. "It's always one of them that provides motivation for the worst kind of human behavior."

"In this case, it was two out of three," Tallon pointed out. "Tisdale still lusted after his wife and he was greedy enough to think money could win her back."

"Crazy stuff," Wyman said. "The whole office is shattered. Giles, Steele and Tisdale, all dead. We lost the entire leadership of the NY office."

"What's that saying – the only thing constant is change?" Pauling asked.

Tallon raised his glass.

"Let's drink to changes – for the better," he said.

The sound of their crystal clinking together sounded like music.

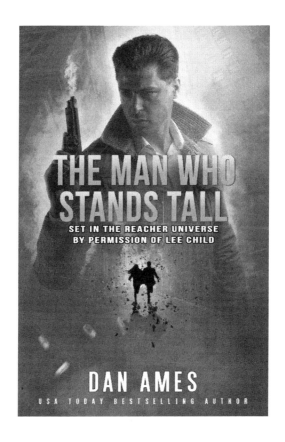

THE MAN WHO STANDS TALL

SET IN THE REACHER UNIVERSE
BY PERMISSION OF LEE CHILD

DAN AMES

USA TODAY BESTSELLING AUTHOR

A USA TODAY BESTSELLING BOOK

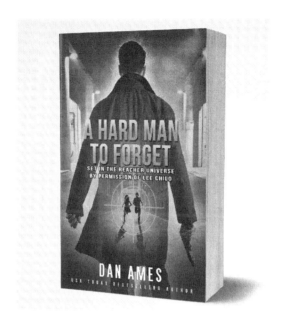

Book One in The JACK REACHER Cases

BOOK ONE IN A THRILLING NEW SERIES

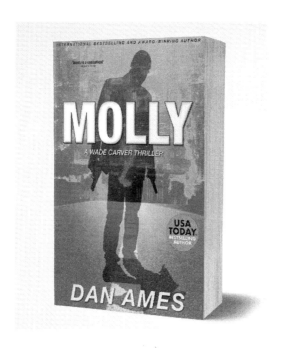

A Blazing Hot New Mystery Thriller Series!

ALSO BY DAN AMES

MURDER WITH SARCASTIC INTENT (Mary Cooper Mystery #2)

GROSS SARCASTIC HOMICIDE (Mary Cooper Mystery #3)

KILLER GROOVE (Rockne & Cooper Mystery #1)

BEER MONEY (Burr Ashland Mystery #1)

THE CIRCUIT RIDER (Circuit Rider #1)

KILLER'S DRAW (Circuit Rider #2)

TO FIND A MOUNTAIN (A WWII Thriller)

STANDALONE THRILLERS:

THE RECRUITER

KILLING THE RAT

HEAD SHOT

THE BUTCHER

BOX SETS:

AMES TO KILL

GROSSE POINTE PULP

GROSSE POINTE PULP 2

TOTAL SARCASM

WALLACE MACK THRILLER COLLECTION

SHORT STORIES:

THE GARBAGE COLLECTOR

BULLET RIVER

SCHOOL GIRL

HANGING CURVE

SCALE OF JUSTICE

Made in the USA
Columbia, SC
12 November 2020

24364531R00086